T0002034

GALATEA

ALSO BY MADELINE MILLER

The Song of Achilles
Circe

GALATEA

A SHORT STORY

MADELINE MILLER

ecco

An Imprint of HarperCollins*Publishers*

Available from HarperCollins e-books
Discover great authors, exclusive offers, and more at hc.com.

Cover design by Allison Saltzman
Cover art © White Snow/Shutterstock

HarperCollins books may be purchased for educational, business, or
sales promotional use. For information, please email the Special Markets
Department at SPsales@harpercollins.com.

Ecco® and HarperCollins® are trademarks of HarperCollins Publishers.

Originally published as an e-book in 2013 by Ecco Books and
Bloomsbury Publishing.

First hardcover edition published in the United Kingdom in 2022 by
Bloomsbury Publishing.

FIRST U.S. HARDCOVER EDITION

Library of Congress Cataloging-in-Publication Data has been applied for.

ISBN 978-0-06-328051-9

22 23 24 25 26   WOR   10 9 8 7 6 5 4 3 2

Galatea

It was almost sweet the way they worried about me.

"You're so pale," the nurse said. "You must keep quiet until your color returns."

"I'm always this color," I said. "Because I used to be made of stone."

The woman smiled vaguely, pulling up the blanket. My husband had warned her that I was fanciful, that my illness made me say things that would sound strange to her.

"Just lie back and I'll bring you something to eat," she said. She had a mole on the side of her lip and I liked to watch it while she talked. Some moles are beautiful and distinctive, like dappling on a horse. But some have hairs in them, and look pulpy like worms and hers was this kind.

"Lie back," she repeated, because I hadn't.

"You know what I think would be good for my color? A walk," I said.

"Oh no," she said. "Not until you're better. Feel how chilled your hands are?"

"That's the stone," I said, "like I told you. It can't get warm without sun. Haven't you ever touched a statue?"

"You're chilled," she repeated. "Just lie back, and be good." She was rushing a little by then, because I had mentioned the stone twice, and this was gossip for the other nurses, and a breathless reason to speak to the doctor. They were fucking, that's why she was so eager. I could hear them sometimes through the wall. I don't say this in a nasty way, for I don't begrudge her a good fuck, if it was good, which I don't know. But I say this so that you understand what I was up against: that I was worth more to her sick than I was well.

The door closed, and the room swelled around me like a bruise. When she was here, I could pretend it felt small because of her, but when she left the four wood walls seemed to press toward me, like lungs that had breathed in. The window did not help, for it was too high to see from the bed, and too small to take in much air. The room smelled sweet and sour at once, as though a thousand suffering people had lain sweating in it, which, I suppose, they had, and then ground roses into the floor with dirty feet.

The doctor was next, and he made noises at me. "Chloe says you have not been lying quietly."

I said, "I'm sorry."

He liked that, but he was also suspicious, because I had been apologizing to him every day for a year. For his sake, I tried to vary it—looking down, biting my lip, twisting my fingers. Once, I burst into tears, and that had been his favorite time. I was working on trying to faint, but didn't have it quite right yet, for I needed to spend a long time breathing very fast first, and I hadn't had enough warning that he was coming. But as soon as I did, that would be the new best time. And the doctor would tell my husband, who would shower him with golden coins, and everyone would be happy, except for me. Though I supposed I would be a little happy, for thinking of it.

"What are you doing?" he said, severely. "This is exactly why you are ill."

I had got up, you see, while I was thinking about the fainting. The room was smallest of all with the doctor in it, and he had had garlic that day, and what smelled like every day he'd ever lived, so I had gone to breathe by the window.

"I'm sorry," I said. "I just love the scent of the narcissus." It was the first thing I thought of, but it only made him frown more, because there were no flowers here, since we are on the rocky edge of a cliff over the sea, so that if I tried to climb out the window, I would not escape but die. Also, I was not even sure narcissus had a smell.

"Lie down this instant," he said. Then, when I obeyed, he took my wrist and held it. "Your pulse is slow," he said.

Of course my pulse is slow, because I used to be made of stone, but I didn't say that. I just made a sound, mmm, that tried to be contrite and interested at once. I thought that if I'd started breathing fast the moment the nurse had closed the door, this might have been the time I could faint. But I had not done it, and now it was too late.

I said, "I think I would feel better if I could walk."

"You are too weak," the doctor said. "What would I tell your husband if you hurt yourself?"

"I used to be stone," I said. "I can't hurt myself from just a walk."

"That's enough," he said, in that voice that meant he was going to send for the tea. The tea is the thing they give me when I won't lie back, and I hate it, for they sit beside me until I drink it all, and then my head aches and my tongue hurts and I piss the bed.

I lay back. "You're right, this is better," I said. "Mmmm, that feels good." Through my lashes I watched him. He was suspicious, so I snuggled down closer. "You're right, I was so tired and I didn't know it." I hoped that this was enough to save me from the tea.

"Be sure you stay there," he said. "Your husband's coming to see you today." And I thought: I should have saved the snuggling bit, because they don't give me the tea when my husband comes. He hates the smell of piss, and he likes me to be able to use my tongue.

I lay down and arranged myself in the right way. It's easy, because I've had a lot of practice, but also because I think there's some part of me, the stone part, that remembers and is glad to settle into solid lines. The only hard thing is the fingers, which my husband likes to say he spent a year on, making them look real instead of still and limp, like lazy sculptors do. So I have to concentrate and hold them just the way he likes, or it ruins everything.

Time passed, I wasn't sure how much. Then through the door I heard the jingle of coins, and the nurses exclaiming. My husband is quite rich now, and has enough to pay for a thousand more doctors who all tell me to lie down. He is rich because of me, if you want to know, but he doesn't like it when I say that. He says it's the goddess's gift first, and then his own since he was the one who made me from the marble. After I was born—and maybe that is not the right word, but if not, then I don't know what is. Woke? Hatched? No, that is worse. I am not an egg.

I will say born. After I was born, he tried to keep me inside as much as he could, but there were servants, and people began to talk about the sculptor's wife, and how strange she was, and how such beauty comes only from the gods. Some people believed him, and some didn't, but suddenly they all wanted statues from him. So he chiseled maiden after maiden, and I said, do you think any of them will come to life? And he said, of course not, these people are not worthy of the goddess's gift. And he told me again how well he had cared for me, dressing me in silks, and draping me in flowers and jewels, and bringing me seashells and colored balls, and praying to the goddess every night. Would not it have been easier to marry a girl from the town? I asked. Those sluts, he said, I would not have them.

The door opened. "Leave and do not disturb us," my husband said to the maids, which was unnecessary, since they've never disturbed us, not in a year's time. But my husband thinks himself a potentate these days.

There was silence, because he was looking at me, checking my fingers and all the rest. I didn't open my eyes, because my job was to lie on the couch without moving so that he might murmur, "Ah, my beauty is asleep." A few times in the past, I had let out a little snore at that moment, just for verisimilitude. But he did not like that at all.

"Asleep?" He said. He stepped into the room. "I am a fool to say so. She is marble and nothing more." He knelt beside the bed, and lifted his hands. "O goddess! Why cannot I find a maiden such as this for my wife? Why must such perfection be marble and not flesh? If only she might—" abruptly, he covered his eyes. "No, I cannot say it."

I thought about making a little snore right then, but that would have been even worse than before.

"I dare not say what I desire. But O, great goddess, you know my secret heart.

I beg you, release me from this torment."
His head slumped to the pallet, and I
opened my eyes, because he couldn't see
me while he wallowed in the covers. His
hair was thinning, and I counted the
bare spots on his scalp. Three, like always.

I closed my eyes, just in time. His head
lifted, and he said, "No, it cannot be. I
must resign myself." But his hand had
fallen conveniently against my forearm,
and he pressed it a little in his agony.

"What is this?" He stared at my arm.
"Can it be? I would swear that she is
warm."

Warmer than regular stone, anyway.

He shook his head, as though to clear

it. "No, I am imagining things. Or perhaps the sun has fallen on her, and warmed the marble."

There was no sun in the room, of course, but it wasn't the time to say this.

"Goddess, do not let me be mad!" He began kneading my hips and belly, hard, testing my stoniness. I prided myself on not flinching.

"Yet I will swear it, I will swear on my life, she is warm. O goddess, if this is a dream, let me still sleep." And then he pressed his lips onto mine. "Live," he said. "Oh live, my life, my love, live."

And that's when I'm supposed to open my eyes like a dewy fawn, and see him poised over me like the sun, and make a little gasping noise of wonder and gratitude, and then he fucks me.

After, I lay against his damp shoulder. I said, "My love, I miss you."

He said nothing, but I could feel his impatience. The sweat was drying on his front, and his back was a swamp. Also, the reed ticking scratched through the sheet, and he's used to a padded bed at home.

"What are you working on?" I asked. Because it is the one thing I know he will answer.

"A statue," he said.

"Ah!" I closed my eyes. "I wish I could see it, darling. What is it of?"

"A girl."

"It will be beautiful," I said. "Is she for one of the men in town?"

"No," he said. "I'm tired of those. This one is for myself."

"How wonderful," I said. "I hope I may see it when you are finished."

"Maybe," he said.

"I will be so good," I said.

He said nothing.

"How old is the girl?" I asked.

"Ten," he said.

I had expected him to say "young." When I had once asked him how old he meant for me to be, he had said, "A virgin."

"Ten," I said. "Not twelve, perhaps?"

"No," he said.

"I do love girls at fifteen," I said. "The other day the nurse brought her daughter, and she was so beautiful. Her whole face was filled with light."

"I have no interest in fifteen," he said. "Or the nurse's daughter."

"Of course not." I stroked his chest with my perfect fingers. I tried to make my voice loose and easy, like a yawn. "How is Paphos, my love?"

"Fine," he said. Just that ugly, nothing word.

"Is she happy?"

"How could she be, after what her mother did?"

I was ready for this, and tipped the tears onto his chest. "I am so sorry, my darling. I wish I could make it up to her."

He pushed me off him and sat up. "You grovel for her, but not me."

I wanted to say, what do you think I have been doing? But of course, my husband would not appreciate that. He is a man who likes white, smooth surfaces. I knelt on the floor, my hands pressed together over my breasts. "My love, there is nothing more in the world I want than to come home with you. Just today I wished that I had something of you to comfort me. A painting, maybe. A painting of you."

This surprised him. "A painting," he said. "Not a statue."

"Oh my darling, a statue would torment me too much," I said. "It would be too much like you to bear."

"Mmm," he said. I let my hands fall a little, so that he might see my breasts better. They were very fine, he had made sure of it.

"Do you not miss me? Even a little?"

"It is your own fault, if I do."

"It is, I know, I know it is. I'm so sorry, darling. I was such a fool, I don't even know what I was doing."

"A fool," he said. He was looking at my breasts again.

"Yes, a terrible fool. An ungrateful fool."

"You should not have run," he said.

"I will never run again, I swear on my life. I can barely stand when you leave me; I live every day yearning for you to come. You are my husband, and father."

"And mother," he said.

"Yes, and mother. And brother too. And lover. All of these."

He said, "You say this only because you want to see Paphos."

"Of course I want to see her. What kind of mother would I be, if I did not? Cold, and shameless. That is not how you and the goddess made me."

I was breathing very hard, but trying to pretend I was not. The floor was hurting my knees, but I did not move.

"Shameless," he said.

"Shameless," I said.

I felt him looking at me, admiring his work. He had not carved me like this, but he was imagining doing it. A beautiful statue, named The Supplicant. He could have sold me and lived like a king in Araby.

He frowned, pointing. "What is that?"

I looked down at my belly and saw the faint silvery tracks on my skin, caught in the light.

"My love, it is the sign of our child. Where the belly stretched."

He stared. "How long have they been there?"

"Since she was born." Ten years ago, now.

"They are ugly," he said.

"I'm so sorry, my love. It is the same for all women."

"If you were stone, I would chisel them off," he said. Then he turned and left and after a little while the doctor came with the tea.

The thing is, I don't think my husband expected me to be able to talk. I don't blame him for this exactly, since he had known me only as a statue, pure and beautiful and yielding to his art. Naturally, when he wished me to live, that's what he wanted still, only warm so that he might fuck me. But it does seem foolish that he didn't think it through, how I could not both live and still be a statue. I have only been born for eleven years, and even I know that.

I conceived that very first time, a moment after I was born. And though I had been stone, and though the goddess made me, my pregnancy was real enough, and I was tired and sick and my feet were too swollen for the delicate golden sandals he liked to see them in. It made him angry,

but it did not stop him from pushing me
onto the bed or up against the wall, and I
worried that because of it I would have
not one child, but a whole litter at once,
like the cats in the street.

My daughter was beautiful and stone-
pale and born in a summer that was so
viciously hot the calves died in the fields.
But she and I were always perfectly cool,
rocking in our chair together. When we
would go walking, everyone whispered
but no one would speak to us, except
once an old woman touched Paphos's foot
and asked for my blessing. I murmured
something, and she touched my arm in
thanks. Her fingers were strange, like

twigs on bare trees, but her skin was very soft.

Sometimes, when my husband was working, we were allowed to go as far as the hillsides. Paphos was older by then, and she would pretend to be a shepherd, and I would pretend to be her sheep. She liked that. She liked it even better when I was a goat, and leapt barefoot from rock to rock, and never wobbled. When she got older still, I insisted on a tutor, though my husband thought that would ruin her. No, I said, she will be useful to her husband, as I am not. And he had smiled at me. You are useful enough. But he hired the tutor in the end, because I fawned on him every time he mentioned it.

In the countryside, Paphos would teach me. Look, she would say, you can use sticks for the letters, and I would say, But some of them are round. And she frowned and said, You're right, shall we go to the beach and use sand? So we did, and it was better than sticks, and even better than the tutor's tablet, because the sea washed it for you. She was a bright girl, very bright, and I didn't have to tell her to say nothing to her father.

At night, my husband sent her to bed. He would say, and you too, wife, are you not sleepy? And I would know it was time to go arrange myself in bed, so that we might pretend again that I was waking from the stone to him.

When Paphos was eight, he sent the tutor away. "He was looking at you," he said to me.

I was distracted that day, thinking of Paphos and the letters, and I said, "Of course he was." Everyone looked at me, because I was the most beautiful woman in the town. I don't say this to boast, because there is nothing in it to boast of. It was nothing I did myself.

My husband stared at me, and said, "You knew?"

I tried to explain, but it was too late. We were not allowed to walk anymore, and Paphos was given a governess instead of a tutor, and her tablets were taken away, and during the days my husband sulked over his marble and did not work. At night, he was rougher than he had been and would not stop asking, Would you be like the rest of them? And I knew to say no, no darling, never.

Paphos was impatient—she hated our house, and wanted our old adventures in the country. She wasn't quiet when her father wished to brood, which was always, and as the days passed she grew more impatient still. I took her to our room and we made the letters with our fingers. She was laughing, and I was too, and we did not know how loud we were.

My husband came to the doorway. "Why are you laughing?"

Paphos said, "Why not?" She was taller than the other girls, and long-limbed. She wasn't afraid of him.

I said, "Darling, I'm so sorry we disturbed you."

"She does not say she is sorry."

"She is still a baby," I said.

"I'm not a baby," Paphos said.

"Then apologize," he said.

"You poor thing, you look half-starved," I said to him. "Have you not eaten?

Paphos, sweetheart, let me talk to your father a moment."

She left, and I saw him grind his teeth at how obediently she did it. He said, "You love her more than me."

Of course not, of course not. My hands stroked his hair, long and greasy from brooding. It is only that she is too smart for that governess, I said. She is bored, and I cannot teach her anything. She needs a tutor.

He said, a tutor.

And I said, yes, another tutor would make everything better, and then we would not bother you. He was quiet, and

I hoped he was considering it, but when I saw his face it was taut and angry, as though he would break the skin. He seized my arm, and he said, you never blush.

I couldn't think to speak, that is how hard he held me.

He said, you do not blush anymore, that is the thing. You apologize and apologize, but you do not blush. Are you shameless now?

No, never, I said. He grabbed the neck of my dress and yanked, but he was not as strong as he wished to be, and it did not tear. He yanked again and again, then pushed me to the floor and held me there, yanking, until the fabric gave way and I was naked.

I covered myself with my hands, and made soft noises like a child. Blush, blush, I prayed. Blush for him, or he will kill you. And I was fortunate, for it was warm in the room, and I was angry, and ashamed too, for I feared that Paphos could hear us, and the blood came to my cheeks and I blushed.

He said, "So you are not completely lost to me." And he sent me to bed, and after, in the torchlight, he wondered at the marks on me, the red around my neck, and the purple on my arms and chest where he had gripped me. He rubbed at them, as though they were stains, not bruises. "The color is perfect," he said, "Look." And he held up the mirror so I could see. "You make the rarest canvas, love."

I had a little money, coins my husband had dropped from his messy purses, things I had found in the street. I had shoes that I stole from the governess, leather things, not gold, that were meant for traipsing up and down dusty roads. I had a cloak that I stole from my husband. Paphos had her own, because I had insisted she got cold easily, though she was like me, and was never cold, nor hot either. And I said to her, "Shall we go to the countryside?"

And she said, "Daddy will not let us," and I said, "I know, so let's not tell him."

We did not make it beyond the next town, because everyone noticed us. "A woman and a girl, pale as milk? Yes, just that way."

The nurse let me lie in the wet for a long time before she came with the dry linens. She bunched the mattress reeds so that they stuck at me worse than ever, and refused to answer me, no matter what I said to her, even when I told her how beautiful her mole was. I wasn't even lying. At that moment it seemed to have a handsomeness of its own.

After, she gave me a bath. She didn't use a cloth, just her hand, dipped in the water. I think she hoped that I would complain about it, but I didn't, because it must be a miserable thing to wash people if you hate it. Next came the rose oil that my husband pays extra for, which she put on as though she was making bread, slapping my skin with both hands. She meant it to hurt, but I sort of liked the vigor of it, the sound and the way my skin went pink.

When she was gone, I wiped off as much of the rose oil as I could on the sheets. The tea had passed through me and my head was clear. I thought: my daughter is ten. Paphos is ten.

The next day, the doctor frowned at me. "Are you unwell?"

"No," I said. "I am very well."

He was about to say, "Then why are you lying down?" but that would have meant admitting that I was not sick to begin with. Ha, I thought.

"I am feeling so calm," I said. "Calm, and well."

"Hmmm," he said.

"I hope my husband comes today," I said. "I miss him terribly."

"He said he would," the doctor said.

"How wonderful," I said. "What wonderful news."

The jingling came late, but I wasn't impatient. I arranged myself just so. The door opened, and my husband sent the nurses away. I heard the lock catch.

"Ah, my beauty is asleep."

And I said, "No, I'm not."

He said, "For your sake, I tell you to lie down, and I will return in a moment when you have collected yourself."

I said, "I am pregnant."

He stared. "It is not possible." Because ever since Paphos, he leaves his seed on my belly.

With the gods, all things are possible, I said. Look at my stomach. I had puffed it a little, so that it looked like a mound. And anyway, he did not know what women looked like. To him, if there was anything, it was strange.

He was pale then, almost as pale as me. "The doctor did not say so."

"I did not show the doctor, I wanted you to be the first to know. Darling, I'm so happy, we shall have another child, and then another after that. And then—"

But the door had already closed. Later the doctor came, with a different kind of tea. He said, you have to drink this. And I said, please, will you send the nurse to sit with me while I do?

He said, all right, for he saw that I would cry otherwise. It was amazing how easy it was.

The nurse came, and I said, will it hurt? I fear it will hurt. And she said, it will hurt a little, and then the blood will come.

I am afraid, I said, and I hid my face in the pillow.

A moment passed, and then I felt her hand on my back. You will be all right, she said. I have done it, and look, I live.

But the baby doesn't live, I said.

No, she said.

I wept, racking, into the cushions.

You must drink the tea, she said. But her voice was not so sharp as usual.

If only I could go outside, I said. I want to give the baby to the goddess.

The doctor doesn't allow it.

I waited, and waited, and wept, and at last she said, but the doctor is not here at night.

I wanted to roll on the grass like a dog, but I was supposed to be pregnant and suffering so I limped, as though every part of me might break. She brought me the tea, and I held it, sipping. She said, tell me when the cramping comes.

I sifted the dirt through my fingers. It was dark, and there was only a little moon, which I took to mean that the goddess, if she existed, smiled on me. I said, I think I feel something. Good, she said. We were in the garden, at the back of the house, away from the sea.

I said, I feel something.

Good, she said.

Then I doubled over, screaming. I fell to the ground, and screamed again. She hesitated, afraid to touch me.

It hurts, it hurts! Get the doctor! She was trembling, and I felt a little sorry, but not sorry enough.

The doctor, yes. I will go for him. Just give me a moment, his house isn't far.

As soon as she was gone, I ran. I did not worry about her catching me. She was clever with her fingers, but she was not fast. I smiled and slipped along the road toward the town.

I did not try the door of the house—I knew it would be locked. But there was a tree behind it, an olive, that Paphos used to beg me to climb with her. I kicked off my sandals and stepped up the warm, gray branches. I reached, and pulled myself into her window.

I had thought about it all day, if I would wake her, or if I wouldn't. But seeing her asleep, I could not. She was a child, only ten, and it would frighten her. So I found the pot of sand she liked to keep because it smelled of the sea and spilled a little on the floor. Paphos, I spelled. I would have said more, but that was most of what I knew.

I slipped from her room, and went to the front door, which was bolted. I did not have to hurry, because no one would look for me here; had I not run from him before? I eased up the bolt and left the door open, a little.

My husband's workroom was in the far wing, where the light was best. I stood outside the door and though I wasn't tired anymore from running, my breath was quick. The house was very quiet around me. There were no servants to worry about—my husband did not like them to sleep in the house.

I pushed open the door and saw the girl, glowing in the room's center. I was afraid, though I told myself that she could not wake, and if she did she would not hurt me. Stone, I told myself, because I was shaking a little. She is stone and she will not wake.

I stepped closer and saw her face. It was pale and pearly, her mouth a soft bow. Her eyes were closed, and she was curled on a stone couch. She looked younger than Paphos because she was so small. She was perfection, every inch of her, from the sweet curls of her ribbons to her sandals painted gold. She had no scabs, and no sand beneath her fingernails. She did not chase the goats, and she did not disobey. You could almost see the flush on her cheeks.

There were silks on her, draped like blankets, and I slipped them off. There was a bracelet of flowers on her wrist, and

I pulled it away. I kissed her forehead and whispered, "Daughter, I'm sorry."

I went to my husband's room, and stood in the doorway. He was flung across the bed, and rumpled.

"Ah, my beauty is asleep," I said.

My husband's eyes opened and he saw me. I turned and ran. I heard a crash as he tripped over the stool I had left for him in the hall, but then he was up again, almost on the stairs. I fled through the front door, and onto the road, and his footsteps slapped behind me. He did not shout, because he didn't want to waste his breath; it was just the night's silence and the two of us, running through the streets. My lungs ached a little but it didn't matter, because I wouldn't need them soon.

The road passed through the town and dipped toward the sea. I was slow and fat from a year of lying in bed, but he had never loved exercise, and was fat and slow himself. The dirt gave way to sand, cool and thick beneath my feet, and then I was on the pebbles, which had never hurt me, and then, at last, the waves. I threw myself in, fighting past the breakers to the open sea. A moment later, I heard the splash of him following.

Water was not my element. It dragged at my clothes as I swam. A little further, I told myself. I could hear him coming, his arms stronger than mine from a lifetime of lifting marble. I felt the water shiver near my foot where he had grabbed and almost caught me. I looked back, and saw how close he was and how far the shore behind. Then his hand seized my ankle and yanked, pulling me to him like a rope, hand over hand, and then he had me up and by the throat, his face pressed to mine.

I think he expected me to fight and claw. I didn't fight. I seized him close around the ribs, holding my wrists so he could not get free. The sudden weight pulled us both under. He kicked and flailed back to the surface, but I was heavier than he had thought, and the waves slopped at our mouths. Let it be now, I prayed.

At first I thought it was just the cold of the water. It crept up my fingers and my arms, which stiffened around him. He struggled and fought, but my hands were fused together and nothing he tried could break them. Then it was in my legs too, and my belly and my chest, and no matter how he kicked, he could not haul us back up to the air. He hit at me, but it was watery and weak and I felt nothing, just the solid circle of my arms, and the inexorable drag of my body.

He had no chance, really. He was only flesh. We fell through the darkness, and the coolness slid up my neck and bled the color from my lips and cheeks. I thought of Paphos and how clever she was. I thought of her stone sister, peaceful on her couch. We fell through the currents and I thought of how the crabs would come for him, climbing over my pale shoulders. The ocean floor was sandy and soft as pillows. I settled into it and slept.

Afterword

Dear Reader,

Galatea is a small morsel, but nevertheless very dear to me. Like its big siblings, The Song of Achilles and Circe, Galatea was inspired by Greek myth, but its method and sensibility were distinct. In Circe and Achilles I drew on many traditions, cross-referencing and interweaving multiple sources. Galatea was a response, almost solely, to Ovid's version of the Pygmalion myth in the Metamorphoses.

Ovid's story goes like this: the sculptor Pygmalion is horrified by seeing prostitutes, whom he condemns as "obscene" and "shameless." He is so disgusted that he spurns all female companionship and instead begins to carve a woman out of ivory. He makes her more perfect than a real woman could be, and falls in love with her. Ovid lingers over descriptions of Pygmalion stroking the statue's body, kissing it, caressing it with his fingers. At last, he prays to the goddess Venus, and she brings the ivory woman to life. Pygmalion embraces her, and the woman, feeling his kisses, blushes deeply (in contrast to the prostitutes who began the story, who are incapable of blushing). The two marry, and produce a child. They live, theoretically, happily ever after.

Ovid's Pygmalion story has a rich history of adaptation in music, dance, poetry, film, and literature. Poets Carol Ann Duffy and H.D. both wrote back to it, as did George Bernard Shaw, whose play *Pygmalion* was the source for *My Fair Lady*. Like much of Ovid's work, the story itself is a bit slippery. For one thing, it's actually a story within a story, narrated by a bitter and grief-stricken Orpheus. Many have seen romance in it: numerous makeover movies, like *Pretty Woman*, clearly owe it a debt. Others have seen it as a metaphor for how artists fall in love with their art. Still others (myself included) have been disturbed by the deeply misogynist implications of the story. Pygmalion's happy ending is only happy if you accept a number of repulsive ideas: that the only good woman is one who has no self beyond pleasing a man, the fetishization of female sexual purity, the connection of the "snowy" ivory with perfection, the elevation of male fantasy over female reality. Galatea does not speak at all in Ovid's version. Even more tellingly, she is not given a name—that was one of the few details I took from other sources. She is only called *the woman*. She is meant to be a compliant object of desire and nothing more.

Galatea broke through when I was working on *Circe*. Although the two women are different in many ways, their stories both center around transformation, on finding freedom for yourself in a world that denies it to you. Galatea's voice came to me late one night in a lightning bolt. I had been trying to fall asleep when the character and the first sentences of her story popped whole into my mind. I sat up and started typing.

From the beginning I knew that *Galatea* was not in the same strictly mythological world as *Circe* and *The Song of Achilles*. She demanded her own world, and in creating it I drew inspiration from many works of feminist literature, as well as Ovid's own love of boundary-crossing and genre-mixing. From there the character continued to grow—I loved her startling matter-of-factness, her cleverness and her courage, her complexity, her ability to keep her sanity and still offer love to her daughter.

As for Pygmalion, I accepted him exactly as Ovid made him. The term "incel" wasn't in wide circulation when I wrote this, but Pygmalion is certainly a prototype. For millennia there have been men who react with horror and disgust to women's independence, men who desire women yet hate them, and who take refuge in fantasies of purity and control. What would it be like to live with such a man as your husband? There are too many today who could answer that. But that is the mark of a good source myth; it is water so wide it can reach across centuries.

I hope you enjoyed the swim.

About the Author

MADELINE MILLER is the author of *The Song of Achilles*, which won the 2012 Orange Prize for Fiction, now known as the Women's Prize for Fiction, and was short-listed for the 2013 Stonewall Book Award in Literature, an instant *New York Times* bestseller, and translated into twenty-five languages. Miller holds an MA in classics from Brown University, and she taught Latin, Greek, and Shakespeare to high school students for over a decade. Her second novel, *Circe*, was a number one international bestseller and short-listed for the 2019 Women's Prize for Fiction.

madelinemiller.com